PLAY THE PART

DOCTORS AND NURSES

Written by Liz Gogerly

Photographs by Chris Fairclough

First published paperback in 2015
by Wayland

Copyright © Wayland 2015

Wayland, an imprint of
Hachette Children's Group
Part of Hodder & Stoughton
Carmelite House
50 Victoria Embankment
London EC4Y 0DZ

Editor: Paul Humphrey
Design: D. R. ink
Commissioned Photography: Chris Fairclough

Dewey Number: 362.1-dc22
ISBN 978 0 7502 9705 9
Library ebook ISBN: 978 0 7502 7262 9

10 9 8 7 6 5 4 3 2 1

MIX
Paper from
responsible sources
FSC® C104740
FSC
www.fsc.org

Printed in China

An Hachette UK Company
www.hachette.co.uk
www.hachettechildrens.co.uk

Picture credits: Liverpool Children's Hospital: p. 7;
Shutterstock Images: pp. 4 (Monkey Business Images),
5 (Wavebreak Media Ltd), 6 (Girish Menon),
12 top (Zurijeta),
12 bottom (Jaimie Duplass).

Contents

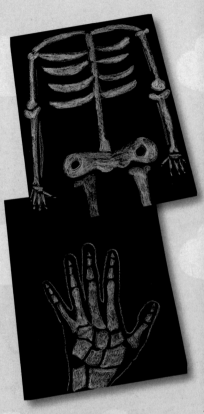

Things to make and do

Play the part

What do doctors and nurses do?

Doctors and nurses have the important job of taking care of our health. They look after us when we get ill. They also give us advice on how to get well again. Sometimes the doctor will **prescribe** some medicine. If someone is seriously ill they may need to go to hospital. There, a team of doctors and nurses work together to make people better.

Doctors and nurses also help us to stay healthy. They give us **vaccinations** to protect us from **disease**. Sometimes, they give us advice about **diet** and exercise.

Dress like a doctor or a nurse

It is important that doctors and nurses wear clothes that are easy to keep clean. Doctors and nurses wear scrubs. Scrubs are a bit like pyjamas with loose tops and trousers. You can make your own scrubs using an old shirt and tracksuit bottoms. You can wear the shirts backwards to look like scrubs!

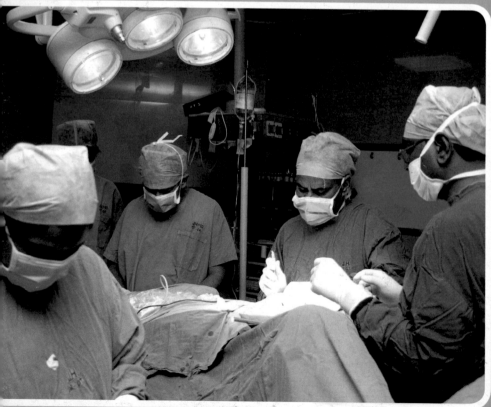

Many doctors at local **surgeries** wear their own clothes. Nurses usually wear a simple uniform. If you want to play the part of a doctor or a nurse there are some great dressing-up clothes you could buy in the shops.

A medical bag

Doctors and nurses sometimes carry a medical bag. Inside there is **medical equipment** that doctors can use to help make people better. You can buy a toy medical bag filled with all the kit you need. It's also fun to make equipment to put in your own bag.

You will need:

★ An empty briefcase, small sports bag or plastic case

★ Plasters

★ Cotton wool

★ A roll of toilet paper to use as bandages or real bandages

★ Small plastic bottles to be used as pretend medicine bottles

★ Toy medical equipment, such as a **stethoscope**, a **blood pressure cuff** and **ear scope**

stethoscope

ear scope

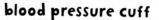

blood pressure cuff

Make a stethoscope that really works!

Listen to your friend's heartbeat with this simple stethoscope.

1 Connect a funnel to each end of the plastic hose using sticky tape.

2 Place one funnel on your friend's chest.

3 Put the funnel at the other end of the hose to your ear.

4 Move the funnel on your friend's chest until you can hear their heartbeat.

The doctor's surgery

When a person feels ill they usually go to see their doctor. Most doctors have a surgery or work in a **health centre**. Doctors, nurses and other staff are all there to help. Visitors to the surgery go to **reception**. Then they sit in the **waiting room** until the doctor or nurse is ready to see them.

Set up your own doctor's surgery

Arrange a **prescription** pad, pens and some medical equipment on the desk. Add the chair. Place the medical bag near the desk. You could make your own posters to decorate the walls. Why not make a colourful poster about eating five portions of fruit and vegetables a day or a poster about how to keep your heart healthy?

You will need:

★ A desk or table
★ A chair
★ A notebook to use as a prescription pad
★ A pen
★ A medical bag
★ Medical equipment, such as a stethoscope, **thermometer**, ear scope and **syringe**
★ Posters for the wall

The children's ward

Sometimes sick or injured people have to go to hospital. Some people have to visit a hospital regularly for **treatment**. If a person goes to hospital for a while they stay on a ward. Most big hospitals have wards just for children. Sometimes the doctors and nurses wear bright uniforms so the children feel more relaxed.

If somebody needs emergency care you should call 999 and ask for an ambulance.

Set up your own children's ward

Push two chairs together to make a hospital bed. Make two more beds in the same way. Arrange the beds into a row like a real hospital ward. Make each bed up with some blankets and a cushion. You could then attach your doctor's notes to the end of each bed using a bulldog clip. Make sure your medical bag is ready for the doctors and nurses to use.

You will need:

* Six chairs
* Six blankets
* Three cushions
* A medical bag
* Three sets of doctor's notes (sheets of paper attached to a piece of cardboard with bulldog clips)

The X-ray machine

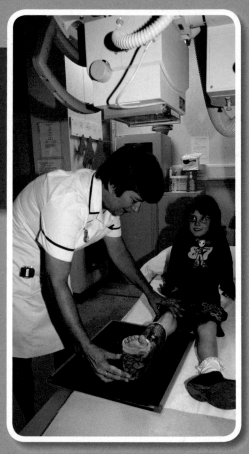

Have you ever fallen over and broken your arm or leg? You probably went to hospital for an X-ray. An X-ray is a photograph of the inside of your body. Doctors can look at the X-ray to see if there is any damage. If a bone is broken then the patient may need to wear a **cast**.

Make your own X-ray photograph

X-ray photographs are taken using an X-ray machine. You can make a simple X-ray machine and X-ray photographs to use for role plays.

1. Take a sheet of black paper. Place a hand on the paper and draw around it with white chalk.

2. Draw some bones inside the outline of the hand. This is your first X-ray photograph.

3. Make more X-ray photographs by drawing other parts of the body and drawing the bones.

You will need:
....
★ Sheet of A4 black paper
★ White chalk

Make your own X-ray machine

1 Cut a two-centimetre wide slit across the length of one of the short sides of your box. Ask an adult to help you.

2 Glue the lid to the box.

3 Paint the box, yoghurt pot and the cardboard tube with the grey metallic paint. Leave them to dry.

4 Place the upside-down yoghurt pot over the top of the tube and fasten it with sticky tape.

5 Attach the cardboard tube to the side of the box using sticky tape.

6 Glue the milk container tops to the top of the box to make your X-ray machine controls.

7 In the role play on pages 18–19, you could pull the X-ray photographs through the slit of your X-ray machine.

15

You have set the scene and made some props. Now you can begin to play the part of a doctor or a nurse in these role plays.

A busy day

In a hospital, doctors and nurses see their patients every day. Play the parts of the doctor, nurse and the patients to find out what happens when they make their hospital rounds.

 DOCTOR: (*doctor and nurse visit first bed*) Hello, Ruby, how are you today?

 RUBY: Very tired. My ear is still hurting…

 DOCTOR: We'd better take your temperature.

 NURSE: (*takes Ruby's temperature with the thermometer*) Ruby, you have a fever.

 DOCTOR: Here is some medicine to help. (*nurse gives Ruby two spoonfuls of medicine*)

NURSE: (*doctor and nurse visit second bed*) Hello, Jay.

 JAY: (*with bandage round his head*) Hello, can I go home today?

 DOCTOR: Let's have a look at your head.

(*doctor takes the bandage off*)

 NURSE: The cut has healed very well.

 DOCTOR: I agree. Jay, you can go home.

(*turns to nurse*) Who's next?

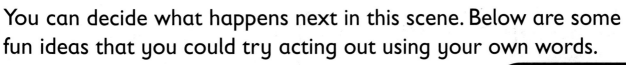

WHAT HAPPENS NEXT?

You can decide what happens next in this scene. Below are some fun ideas that you could try acting out using your own words. Then have a go at making up your own scenes.

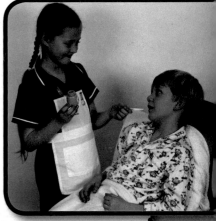

1 The doctor listens to Leo's chest with a stethoscope and says he's still poorly. The nurse gives him some medicine.

2 Leo has a cast on his broken leg. The doctor tells the nurse to remove the cast. Afterwards, Leo says his leg feels much better.

3 Leo is dressed and wants to go home. The nurse looks at his notes. She tells him to get straight back into bed because he has measles.

Oh no, broken bones!

Play the parts of the doctor, the nurse and a child with a broken arm to find out what happens when somebody has an X-ray.

 NURSE: *(to doctor)* Anya has fallen off her bike and may have broken her arm.

 DOCTOR: *(looks at Anya's arm)* Mmm, let's take a look.

 ANYA: Ouch, it hurts when I move it.

DOCTOR: Your arm is swollen. Anya, you need an X-ray.

 ANYA: Oh dear. Will that hurt?

 DOCTOR: You won't feel anything. It's just like having a photograph taken...

WHAT HAPPENS NEXT?

You can decide what happens next in this scene. Below are some fun ideas that you could try acting out using your own words. Then have a go at making up your own scenes.

1 The nurse takes Anya for an X-ray. Anya feels scared and can't stop shaking. The nurse tells her not to worry and to stay still while the X-ray photograph is taken.

2 The doctor looks at the X-ray photograph of Anya's arm. He can't see a break in her arm. He tells Anya she must go home and rest her arm. He gives her a prescription for some medicine so she doesn't feel any pain.

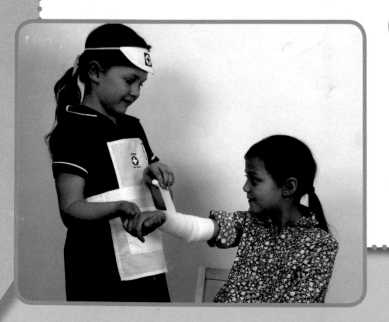

3 The doctor looks at the X-ray photograph of Anya's arm. He tells her she has broken her arm. The nurse puts a cast on the poorly arm and gives her some medicine.

Accident in the doctor's surgery

Play the parts of the doctor and nurse in this role play set at a doctor's surgery. Find out what happens when a boy comes to see the doctor with a bad finger...

 NURSE: (*enters the doctor's surgery*) Good morning, doctor. Your first patient is ready to see you.

 DOCTOR: Who is it?

 NURSE: It's Isaac.

DOCTOR: Send him in.

 ISAAC: Hello, doctor. I cut my finger yesterday. Mum put a plaster on it but it's very red and swollen today.

DOCTOR: Let's have a look, Isaac. (*doctor peels off the plaster*)

ISAAC: Ouch, that hurts!

 DOCTOR: Oh dear. This cut looks infected. How did you cut it?

ISAAC: Playing outside. I cut myself on my dad's old rusty bike.

DOCTOR: OK, Isaac. First we have to take your temperature.

 NURSE: (*nurse takes Isaac's temperature with the thermometer*) It's normal, doctor.

DOCTOR: Right! Now the nurse is going to clean up the cut and put on a new plaster.

 ISAAC: Will it hurt?

(continued over page)

Accident in the doctor's surgery

(continued)

 NURSE: No, your finger is going to feel much better!
(nurse cleans the cut and puts on a new plaster)

 ISAAC: Oh, that *is* much better. Can I go home now?

 DOCTOR: Not yet. You need an injection.
It will get rid of the infection.

 ISAAC: Oh no! Will it hurt?

DOCTOR: Only a little bit.

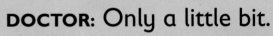

ISAAC: I'm so scared!

 DOCTOR: Try looking away from the needle and count to ten.

 ISAAC: One, two, three, four…

 DOCTOR: It won't take a moment … *(doctor gets the syringe)*

WHAT HAPPENS NEXT?

You can decide what happens next in this scene. Below are some fun ideas that you could try acting out using your own words. Then have a go at making up your own scenes.

1 Isaac says he feels better and doesn't need the injection.

2 The doctor gives the injection. Isaac says 'Ouch'. The nurse tells him he has been very brave and gives him a sticker.

3 The doctor gives the injection. Isaac says it didn't hurt a bit. He gives the doctor and nurse a big thumbs up!

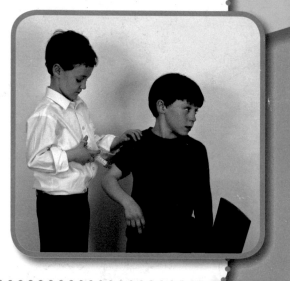

GLOSSARY

blood pressure cuff An instrument that measures how fast a person's blood is being pumped around the body by the heart.

cast A stiff bandage used to support and protect a broken leg or arm.

diet The food that you eat.

disease An illness.

ear scope An instrument doctor's use to look inside a patient's ear.

health centre A building where a group of doctors work.

medical equipment Tools used to treat an illness or injury.

prescribe When a doctor advises a patient to take certain medicine.

prescription A form filled out by the doctor which lists the medicines a patient needs.

reception A place near the entrance of a workplace where visitors ask for information.

stethoscope A device used by doctors to listen to a patient's heart and breathing.

syringe A tube fitted with a needle, used to inject fluids into a person's body.

surgery A place where doctors meet their patients.

thermometer An instrument for measuring a patient's temperature.

treatment Care given to a patient for an illness or injury.

vaccination A substance injected into a patient to protect against disease.

waiting room A place where patients wait to be called to see the doctor.

INDEX